Katie and the Smallest Bear

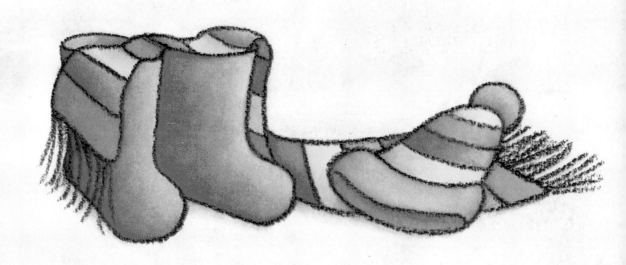

Also illustrated by Emilie Boon:

Peterkin's Wet Walk
Peterkin Meets a Star
Belinda's Balloon

All published by Picture Corgi Books

Katie and the Smallest Bear

Story by
Ruth McCarthy

Pictures by
Emilie Boon

PICTURE CORGI BOOKS

For Steven

KATE AND THE SMALLEST BEAR
A PICTURE CORGI BOOK 0 552 523550

Originally published in Great Britain in 1985 by William Heinemann Ltd.

PRINTING HISTORY
Picture Corgi edition published 1987

Reprinted 1987

Reprinted 1988
Illustrations © Emilie Boon 1985
Text © Ruth McCarthy 1985

Picture Corgi Books are published by Transworld Publishers Ltd., 61-63 Uxbridge Road, Ealing, London W5 5SA, in Australia by Transworld Publishers (Australia) Pty. Ltd., 15-23 Helles Avenue, Moorebank, NSW 2170, and in New Zealand by Transworld Publishers (N.Z.) Ltd., Cnr. Moselle and Waipareira Avenues, Henderson, Auckland.

Printed in Portugal by Printer Portuguesa

The smallest bear was bored. It was a
lovely sunny day and he had nobody
to play with.

Then he saw a little girl looking through the fence at him.

"Hello," she said, "I'm Katie. Will you come and play?"

"Oh yes!" said the smallest bear "I'll come now!"

So he wriggled under the fence to her.
Katie gave him her hat and scarf to wear,

so he looked just like a fat little boy
in a fur coat, and they walked
out of the zoo
along the road
and into the park.

They ran past the ducks,
chased two squirrels up a tree
and rushed into the playground.

There was a swing, a seesaw, a slide and a roundabout.

The smallest bear pushed Katie on the swing – higher and higher and higher – as high as the sky.

Then they went on the seesaw. Up,
down, up, down, UP!

Katie went on the slide first. The smallest bear whizzed down behind her – his slippery fur made him very fast – and he went BUMP at the bottom.

They went on the roundabout together, whirling round and round until Katie felt dizzy, and the smallest bear's hat flew off.

They played and played and played
until Katie said, "I'm hungry; let's go
home for tea."

So they went home to Katie's house, where they had sticky honey sandwiches, bananas and yoghurt and big glasses of orange juice.

"I want to go home now," said the smallest bear when he'd finished his tea.

"All right," said Katie, "I'll take you."
So they walked
out of the house
along the road
and back to the zoo.

"Goodbye," said the smallest bear, "can we play another day?"

"Goodbye," said Katie. "We'll go to the park again soon." And they did.